Contents

1. At Gateshead Hall 5
2. The Red Room 8
3. The Doctor 12
4. Mr. Brocklehurst 14
5. Lowood 17
6. Helen 21
7. Disgrace .24
8. Miss Temple 28
9. Fever 31
10. Leaving Lowood 34
11. Thornfield Hall 37
12. The Horseman 41
13. My Employer 45
14. The Fireside 48
15. Danger 51
16. The Next Day 55
17. Blanche Ingram 58
18. The Stranger 62
19. The Gypsy 64
20. The Cry 68
21. Mrs. Reed 72
22. Back to Thornfield 75
23. Midsummer Eve 77
24. Preparations for a Wedding 81
25. The Veil 84
26. The Wedding 87
27. Decision .92
28. The Moor .95
29. Moor House 98
30. Partings .101
31. Rosamond 103
32. The Portrait 105
33. St. John's News 107
34. Plans for India 111
35. "Jane, Jane, Jane!" 114
36. Back to Thornfield 117
37. At Ferndean 120
38. Afterward 126

1

At Gateshead Hall

It was a cold, wet day in November, so we were indoors. My aunt, Mrs. Reed, was on the fireside sofa in the drawing room with my cousins Eliza, John, and Georgiana around her, but I was not allowed to join them. Mrs. Reed was displeased with me.

"Your behavior is not natural and childlike," she had said, but when I asked her exactly what I had done, she told me I should not question my elders.

At least my cousin John was leaving me alone for a little while. I slipped into the breakfast room next door, chose a book, and curled up on the window seat behind a curtain. I loved books, even when they were difficult to understand, and I was very happy until I heard John's voice.

"Where the dickens is Jane?" he demanded. "She's run off like a naughty animal." I kept very still behind the curtain, but he managed to find me.

I was only ten and he was fourteen – a big, heavy bully. Complaining was no use; he was his mother's favorite. The maids, Bessie and Miss Abbott, knew he was greedy and spoiled, but Mrs. Reed would hear nothing against him.

He grabbed the book from my hands and ordered me out of my hiding place. As always, I was so terrified that I obeyed him. He seated himself, glared at me from his fat, flabby face with its heavy features, stuck out his tongue, and yanked my hair.

"That's for sneaking away," he said. "What were you doing behind the curtain?"

"Reading," I said.

"You have no right to touch the books," announced John. "You ought to beg, and not live here with a gentleman's family like us, and eat the same meals as we do, and wear clothes at our mother's expense. I'll teach you to behave. Stand by the door."

I saw him lift the book to throw it, and I flinched away, but not soon enough; it hit me so hard that I stumbled against the door. There was a sting of pain in my head, and blood trickled down my face.

Anger overcame me. I had never stood up to John before, but this time I screamed out all the things I thought about him until he ran to grab me. I fought him off.

"Rat! Rat!" he shouted, and yelled for help. My aunt and the maids rushed in.

"Poor Master John!" cried the servants.

"Take her to the red room!" ordered Aunt Reed. "Lock her in!"

2

The Red Room

Until then I had always tried not to be troublesome, but this time Bessie and Miss Abbot had to drag me away. Expecting some terrible punishment, I screamed and fought.

"How shocking!" scolded Miss Abbot. "Striking your master!"

"He is not my master!" I screamed as they bundled me into the red room. "I'm not a servant!"

"No, you're less than a servant, for you do nothing to earn your keep," said Bessie, pushing me on to a stool. "Will you sit still, or do we have to tie you?"

I could not bear such a disgrace, so I gripped the stool and promised not to move. They stood back, folding their arms and frowning at me.

"Mrs. Reed is very kind to you," Bessie reminded me. "You would have no home, if not for her."

"You should not think yourself equal to your cousins," said Miss Abbot. "They will have a great deal of money and you will have none. It is your place to be humble and pleasant."

"What we tell you is for your own good," added Bessie more gently. "If you are bad tempered and rude, you may be sent away."

"Hang your head and be sorry," said Miss Abbot, "or something bad might come down the chimney and get you!"

Then they went away, locking me in.

The red room was enormous, shrouded in crimson curtains. All was dark wood and deep red furnishings except for the ghostly white covers on the bed. The furniture was impressive, but the room was lonely, gloomy, and cold. It had hardly been used since my Uncle Reed had died there, nine years before.

Why did they all hate me so much? Eliza was selfish. Georgiana was vain and spiteful. John was cruel, rough, and arrogant. They were all loved and praised, while I, who tried so hard to be good and quiet, was blamed for being disobedient and sullen.

It grew darker and colder, and my courage sank. I thought of Uncle Reed. He had been my mother's brother, and I never doubted that he would have been kind to me, if he had lived. What if his ghost should rise up, angry at the way I was treated? The thought of it brought me no comfort, only a growing terror.

Suddenly, a beam of chilly light gleamed on the wall. It may only have been a lantern outside, but to me, alone in a place of death, it seemed ghostly and terrible. My heart beat fast, my head grew hot, and I thought I would suffocate. Desperately, I rushed to the door, screaming out for help and wrenching at the door handle. At last, Bessie and Miss Abbot came.

"Miss Eyre, are you ill?" asked Bessie. I clung to her hand, and she did not snatch it from me.

"She only screamed to bring us all running," said Miss Abbot.

"What is all this?" demanded another voice. My aunt was striding along the corridor.

"Forgive me, Aunt!" I sobbed. "Please, I can't bear it – I shall die!"

Ignoring my pleas, she flung me, still crying and pleading, back into the red room, and locked the door.

I remember nothing after that. I think I had some sort of fit, and I passed out.

3

🌿 🌿 🌿

The Doctor

I woke feeling as if I had just had a nightmare, but somebody slipped an arm gently around me and helped me sit up. I was in my own bed, and Dr. Lloyd was talking to me, telling me I would be fine. As long as he was beside me, I felt safe. Bessie, too, came and asked me if I wanted anything. All this gentleness astonished me! Nobody had been kind to me before.

I was allowed out of bed the next day, feeling weak and anxious. I did not know what would happen next. Bessie was still kind and sang to me, but the song was a sad one and made me cry.

When the doctor came again, he noticed I had been crying. "Do you like Gateshead Hall? Do you like living here?" he asked, after Bessie had left the room.

"I hate it," I said. "I wish I could get away."

"Would you like to go to school?" he asked.

I knew very little about school, but I knew that girls learned to sing and draw there, and I thought I would like that. Anything must be better than Gateshead Hall.

"Yes, I should like it," I said.

At that moment I heard the carriage on the gravel outside, and Dr. Lloyd, saying he must speak to Mrs. Reed, went away.

Nothing else was said to me that day about school, but I heard Bessie and Miss Abbot talking in the nursery when they thought I was asleep.

"Mrs. Reed will be glad to get rid of Jane Eyre," said Miss Abbot. "That child always looks as if she's plotting something."

"Why is she living here?" asked Bessie. I listened carefully. Nobody had ever told me this.

"Why, her mother was Mr. Reed's sister," said Miss Abbot. "She married a nearly penniless clergyman, and her father was furious and had nothing more to do with her. They went away to work among poor people, caught typhoid, and died when Miss Jane was a baby, so she was sent here."

"Poor little Jane," sighed Bessie.

"Yes, if she were a pretty little darling like Miss Georgiana you'd feel sorry for her," said Miss Abbot. "Shall we go and have supper?"

4

Mr. Brocklehurst

I hoped I would be sent to school immediately, but for months nothing changed, except that Mrs. Reed separated me from her own children more than ever. I had to sleep and eat alone, and stay in the nursery while they were in the dining room. They must have been told to avoid me because that was what they did. During Christmas I was left out of all the parties and presents, but I did not really mind. At least I didn't have to be with my cousins.

One January morning, Bessie gave me a rough and thorough wash, brushed my hair hard, and sent me to Aunt Reed. She was sitting by the breakfast-room fire with a man in black who, with his great height, dark clothes, and grim face looked like a black pillar of stone. My aunt called him Mr. Brocklehurst.

"This is Jane Eyre, Mr. Brocklehurst," she said. "I would like her to begin attending your school at Lowood."

"Come here, Jane Eyre!" he commanded in a deep voice, and glowered down at me from under enormous bushy eyebrows. "Do you obey your elders?"

"Yes, sir."

"Do you like to study books?"

"When I am permitted to choose them."

"What? How very shocking! That proves you have a wicked heart; you must always do as you are told."

Mrs. Reed spoke. "Mr. Brocklehurst, I must warn you of Jane's worst fault," she said. "She tells lies. You must be very strict with her." It seemed she wanted to spoil school for me before I even started – but what could I do? Nothing.

"I wish her to be made useful and kept humble," continued Mrs. Reed. "Also, I insist that she spend all of her vacations at Lowood."

"Of course, Mrs. Reed. She shall most certainly learn to be humble. Why, at Lowood we aim to crush all worldly pride," said Mr. Brocklehurst. "I shall write to Miss Temple, telling her to expect a new girl."

He left. I knew I should go too, but I remembered what Aunt Reed had told him about me. I had to speak!

"I don't tell lies," I burst out suddenly. "If I did I should say I loved you, but I do not. I will never come to see you when I am grown up. If anyone asks me about you, I will tell them how you treated me with miserable cruelty. Send me to school soon, for I hate it here."

"I certainly will," murmured Mrs. Reed, and she rose and left.

Bessie was unusually kind to me in my last days at Gateshead Hall. The last day of all, when she helped me pack, was one of the happiest I had known.

5
🌿 🌿 🌿

Lowood

I left Gateshead Hall on the six o'clock coach, giving Bessie one last hug before we clattered away. Nobody else was there to say good-bye.

We traveled all day and into the night. The coach stopped at last in rain and darkness, so I could see very little of Lowood. A young woman, one of the teachers, came to meet me and hurried me through the corridors until we arrived in a long, wide room full of girls.

They all wore very plain brown dresses and wool stockings, and their hair was combed back severely from their faces. They youngest must have been nine, and the oldest twenty. The teacher, Miss Miller, took her place at the end of the room.

"Monitors!" she called. "Collect the books and fetch the supper trays!"

Four tall girls tidied away the books and brought in supper, which was a little drink of water from a shared mug and a tiny piece of biscuit, but I was too nervous to eat even that. Then we all went to a long room where we slept, two to each bed.

The morning was still dark and bitterly cold when we had to rise, wash shivering in icy water, and go downstairs for early study, which lasted for an hour. Having eaten so little the day before, I felt sick with hunger. Then, at last, we were sent to the dining hall for breakfast.

To my dismay, the breakfast smelled far from pleasant. The girls were wrinkling their noses.

"The porridge is burned again!" whispered someone. It tasted disgusting, and even I, who was starving, could not eat it. We went to our lessons hungry.

We were all taught in a single large schoolroom. I was looking at the teachers – a stout one, a dark and gloomy one, a foreign woman, and Miss Miller – when all the girls stood up. The headmistress was quietly entering the room.

Her name, I discovered, was Miss Temple. She was tall, pale, and dark-haired, and for some minutes she surveyed us gravely and silently. I saw kindness in her eyes and dignity in her bearing.

She spent the morning teaching the older girls, and at twelve o'clock she stood up and addressed the school. "You had a breakfast this morning that you could not eat," she said. "You must be hungry. I have ordered bread and cheese for you all."

The other teachers looked shocked, but we were all delighted. As soon as we had finished the food, we were sent outdoors.

It was freezing and foggy, the ground was soaking, and our thin dresses and cloaks were not enough to keep us warm. Cold, hungry, and alone, I looked at the miserable garden and wondered about my future here.

Close to me, someone coughed. I looked around and saw a girl sitting on a bench, reading. Here was somebody else who liked books! When she looked up we began to talk, and I asked her who the house belonged to.

"Mr. Brocklehurst," she said. "He buys all our food and clothes. Miss Temple is very good and very smart, but Mr. Brocklehurst makes the decisions."

Her name was Helen Burns, and she was an orphan like I was. By the time the dinner bell rang, I had a friend.

Dinner was a repulsive smelling stew, and even though I was hungry I only ate a little. More lessons followed, then tea with a small scrap of bread, studying, the usual supper of dry biscuit and a sip of water, and bed. Such was my first day at Lowood.

6

Helen

The next morning, the washing water was frozen. The porridge was edible, but the portions were tiny.

All the classes met in the same schoolroom, with different lessons taking place. Although I was put into the youngest group I found the lessons hard, and I was glad when, in the afternoon, I was given a piece of sewing to do. Helen Burns was in a different class, but I could hear her teacher, Miss Scatcherd, calling her name all the time. "Burns, hold your head up! Burns, tuck in your chin!"

When the girls had to answer questions it seemed to me that Helen was the only one who had understood the lesson, but Miss Scatcherd still scolded her. "You dirty, disagreeable girl! Why have you not cleaned your nails?"

Helen never said a word to defend herself, even when Miss Scatcherd sent her to fetch a little bundle of twigs called the rod. She curtsied, then stood quietly still while, to my horror, Miss Scatcherd whipped her across the neck with that vicious little rod. My fingers shook with anger, so that I could not go on sewing.

That evening, I talked to Helen. "Why is Miss Scatcherd so cruel to you?"

"She is not cruel," she said simply. "She is trying to correct me."

"If she struck me with that rod, I would take it and break it under her nose," I said.

"If you did, you would be expelled. I am untidy and careless, as she says, so I suppose I deserve it. Besides, it is best to love our enemies and be good to those who hate us."

"If I did that, I would have to love my cousin John and Aunt Reed," I said, "and that would be impossible." I told her all about Gateshead Hall.

"I agree, she has been cruel to you," she said. "However, nursing your anger has not made you any happier. Life is too short for that, Jane. Life is short, and heaven is forever. That is the thing I look forward to, Jane! Heaven!"

She became very quiet and dreamy after this, until one of the monitors, a big rough girl, came and ordered her to tidy her drawer. She obeyed at once, without a word.

7

❧ ❧ ❧

Disgrace

It was a long, harsh winter. We were made to spend an hour of each day outside and walk two miles to town and back every Monday, often in a bitterly cold wind. We had neither gloves nor boots, only thin shoes that let in the snow, and our fingers and toes grew sore. The bigger girls huddled around the schoolroom fire, so we younger ones stayed cold. They took food from us too, and there was little enough to begin with.

One afternoon during an arithmetic lesson, all the girls and teachers suddenly stood up. I did too, and looked up to see Mr. Brocklehurst.

I had dreaded this event. He had believed everything Mrs. Reed had said about me, and how would I bear it if he informed Miss Temple of my bad character? I bent my head over my slate and hoped he would not see me. For the moment he only spoke, gruffly, to Miss Temple.

"I am not pleased with the accounts," I heard him say. "Twice this term the girls have had an extra meal of bread and cheese. Why was that? Who is responsible?"

"Their breakfast was too burned to eat," she replied. "They should not go hungry all day."

"They must not be pampered, madam! They are here to learn patience and self-denial, and so must learn to live with disappointments. If you feed their bodies too well, you will starve their souls."

Miss Temple had turned very white. Her lips were pressed tightly together. Mr. Brocklehurst turned and, with his hands behind his back, surveyed the class.

"There is a girl here with curly hair!" he exclaimed.

"Her hair curls naturally," said Miss Temple.

"Nature! We have nothing to do with nature! Do we want these girls to be vain? All of these girls must have their hair cut short. I will send a barber tomorrow."

At this point, his wife and daughters arrived. I did not think he was worried about any of them becoming vain, for they all wore silk gowns and jewelry and had their hair curled. Still hoping to be unnoticed, I kept my head down, but the slate slipped suddenly from my hand and fell with a terrible crash on the floor.

"A careless girl!" said Mr. Brocklehurst. He added, "The new girl! I must speak to you concerning her. Come forward, child!"

Too terrified to move, I was dragged to the front of the class by two older girls. On Mr. Brocklehurst's orders, they hoisted me on to a high stool.

"Do you see this girl?" he said. Of course they did. The whole school was staring up at me. "She is young and has the face of childhood, but already she is a servant of evil and I must warn you against her. Teachers, watch her and punish her. This girl," he went on, "is – a – liar! She even lied to the generous lady who brought her up!"

With these words and a swish of silk gowns, the Brocklehursts left. Mr. Brocklehurst turned at the door.

"She must stay there for half an hour!" he announced to the class. "Nobody is to speak to her all day!"

I have no words to tell you of the shame I felt, standing up there before the whole school and near to tears. Just as I thought I would break down, Helen Burns came past. She lifted her eyes, and there was a smile of true kindness and understanding that gave me courage.

8

Miss Temple

By the time my half hour was over, the rest of the school had gone. I crept into a corner and cried.

I had just begun to do well at Lowood, and Miss Temple had that day promised to teach me drawing and French. Now, I had been crushed and trampled on. Certain that I would never be happy, I wished to die.

Somebody was coming in. It was Helen, bringing my bread and coffee, but I was crying too hard to eat.

"They all hate me," I sobbed.

"Of course not!" she said. "Nobody likes Mr. Brocklehurst! If he had made a pet of you, that would have turned everyone against you! Besides, Jane, what would it matter if all the world hated you when you know you are innocent?" Then her coughing became so bad, she had to stop talking.

Miss Temple came in and seated herself comfortably beside us.

"Have you finished crying?" she asked.

"Yes, but everyone will think I am a liar now," I said.

"We will believe you to be what you show yourself to be, Jane," she said kindly. "Come to my apartment and tell me your side of the story."

In Miss Temple's room, I told her about Gateshead Hall. When I mentioned our doctor, she nodded.

"I know of him," she said. "I will write to him, and if he agrees with your story the whole school will be told you are innocent. I believe you." Then, sitting with her arm around me, she asked

Helen about her cough, and whether she had any pain. She felt Helen's pulse and looked anxious, but then she smiled, rang a bell, and asked her servant to bring in tea.

Everything was so pretty! We had tea and toast on delicate china, and she even brought out cake for us, which was something we hardly ever saw.

When it was time to go I noticed that she watched Helen sadly, and I saw a tear on my teacher's cheek.

We went immediately back to the bedroom, only to find Miss Scatcherd inspecting each girl's drawer. Helen was severely scolded for the untidiness of her things.

A week later, Miss Temple received a letter from the doctor supporting my version of events at Gateshead Hall. In front of the whole school, she announced that I was innocent of Mr. Brocklehurst's charges against me.

I made a new start. I worked hard and began to study French and drawing, which I greatly loved. Lowood was becoming bearable.

9

❦ ❦ ❦

Fever

Spring arrived, and the weather became kinder. Snowdrops grew in the garden, and the woods brightened with green leaves – but the warmer weather also brought disease. Lowood was struck by typhoid fever. Already undernourished, more than half the girls became sick.

Those who could go home were sent away, though some were already dying. Others died at the school. The teachers had no time to teach, and Mr. Brocklehurst no longer came near Lowood at all, so those of us who were well had almost unlimited freedom. There was more food to go around, and we could take our lunch outside to eat in the woods if we chose to.

Where was Helen? I hardly ever saw her, for she was kept apart from us all. She did not have typhoid, but she was ill with consumption and rarely left Miss Temple's room. I was not sure what consumption was, but I thought it could not be anything dangerous.

One evening, when I had stayed late in the woods, I felt guilty as I came back to Lowood. I was enjoying the woods on a warm June evening, while Helen was shut away and unwell. As I reached the front door, the school nurse was saying good-bye to the doctor, and I ran to her.

"How is Helen?" I asked.

"Very poorly," she replied. "She'll not be here much longer."

For the first time, I understood that Helen was dying. Horror and grief gave way to a great desire to see her, but the nurse would not let me. I went to bed, and lay awake.

When all was quiet, I tiptoed to Miss Temple's room. There, in a little bed, lay Helen. She was pale and thin, but looked so calm that I thought, after all, there was nothing to fear. Her hand, when I took it, felt cold, but she smiled and I was sure she would not die.

"You are just in time to say good-bye, Jane," she said.

"Are you going home?" I asked.

"To my last home," she said.

"No, no!" I cried, but Helen was seized by a violent fit of coughing.

When she could speak again, she said, "Jane, your little feet are bare. Come in beside me and keep warm."

I nestled under the quilt beside her. After a long silence, she whispered, "Don't be upset. We all must die one day. I would not have been happy in the world, so for me, dying young is the best way. I am going to a better place, where everything is good and love is abundant."

"Do you really believe that, Helen?" I said. "Shall I see you when I die?"

"You will, Jane, no doubt," she said.

I held her tightly, with my face against her neck. I wanted to keep her with me.

"I feel so comfortable now," she said. "I think I can sleep. Stay with me, Jane."

"Nobody shall take me away," I said. "Oh, Helen, good night."

"Good night, my dearest Jane," she said, and we fell asleep.

I woke in the morning in somebody's arms. The nurse was carrying me back to my own bed.

Afterward, I was told that Miss Temple had returned to her room to find me asleep in Helen's bed. Helen had died in her sleep beside me.

10

Leaving Lowood

The typhoid finally wore itself out, but news of it, and of the deaths at the school, had traveled. There was an inquiry that brought to light the truth about Lowood with its wretched clothing, poor food, and bad conditions. Mr. Brocklehurst was disgraced. Lowood was put into the care of kind and sensible trustees, and both diet and clothing improved. I stayed for eight more years, six as a pupil and two as a teacher. I grew up small, pale, and plain, but I had an education.

Miss Temple was a friend, mother, and teacher to me, but when I was eighteen she married and left Lowood. It was time for a change. I grew restless, knowing I had seen hardly anything of the world outside school and Gateshead Hall, and I longed for some sort of freedom.

I put an advertisement in the newspaper:

Young woman teacher seeks employment as a governess. French, drawing, and music offered.

A reply came from a lady named Mrs. Fairfax at Thornfield Hall, about seventy miles away. She wanted a governess for a little girl, and the pay was twice as much as my salary at Lowood.

The trustees gave me an excellent reference, but as Mrs. Reed was still my guardian I needed her permission to leave the school. They wrote to her, and she replied, "Jane Eyre may do as she pleases. I want nothing to do with her." I was free to go.

I was much surprised to have a visitor on my last evening at Lowood, when I was packing. Bessie, my aunt's servant, had come all that way to see me before I left! She was now married to the coachman and had brought her little son, Bobby, to see me. She was delighted to find me happy and to see my drawings. She asked me to play the piano, and she insisted that I played better than my cousins.

"How are they?" I asked.

"The young ladies are well, but they're always quarreling. Mrs. Reed is in good health, but Mr. John worries her. He was thrown out of college, and he wastes money terribly. And did you know, miss, that a gentleman came asking about you?"

"What gentleman, Bessie?"

"Your father's brother, Mr. Eyre, miss. He lives in a foreign country now and was visiting England. He was so disappointed when Mrs. Reed said you'd gone away to school, because his ship was to leave London in a day or two, and he didn't have time to look for you. He looked like a real gentleman."

Bessie and Bobby stayed at Lowood that night. The next morning, I set off for whatever awaited me at Thornfield Hall.

11

Thornfield Hall

After sixteen hours of traveling on a raw October day I arrived at Millcote, where the coachman from Thornfield Hall awaited me. During that long journey I had wondered what Mrs. Fairfax might be like, but it was too late for second thoughts.

We arrived at Thornfield in darkness. Only one front window was lit by candlelight, but I was led to a bright, cozy room with a cheerful fire. An elderly lady, very neat in black silk with a snowy white apron, rose to meet me. She clasped my hands warmly.

"Mrs. Fairfax?" I asked.

"Yes, that is right. Do sit by the fire, you must be cold." She summoned a servant. "Leah, fetch Miss Eyre's supper and ask John to put her luggage in her room." I had not expected such friendliness from an employer!

"Shall I see Miss Fairfax tonight?" I asked, thinking of the child I was to teach.

"Miss Fairfax? Oh, you mean Miss Varens," she said. "I have no family. I am so glad you are here! Thornfield was always a lonely place, but now we have little Adele Varens, and Sophie, her maid, and yourself. But you must feel tired. Let me show you to your room."

It was a comfortable room with carpet and papered walls, which I had never had at school. I went to bed feeling safe, happy, and thankful. In the morning Mrs. Fairfax showed me around Thornfield, which turned out to be a gentleman's manor house with woods and gardens.

I discovered that Mrs. Fairfax was not the owner of Thornfield, but the housekeeper. It belonged to a distant relation of hers, Mr. Edward Fairfax Rochester, who was away from home. My pupil Adele, was his ward. Mrs. Fairfax was just explaining that Adele was French when a very pretty, curly-haired child came running across the lawn to meet us. This was my seven-year-old pupil.

"Good morning, Miss Adele," said Mrs. Fairfax. "Come and meet Miss Eyre."

When Adele realized I spoke French she chattered without stopping. Only when she had

gone with her maid to play could I question Mrs. Fairfax about Mr. Rochester.

"He is away from Thornfield a great deal, but he is a good landlord to his tenants," she said, "and well respected."

"Do you like him?" I asked.

"He is a good master, but I can never be sure whether he is pleased or not, and whether he is being serious. He is difficult to understand."

This was all she could tell me of him, and she proceeded to show me more of the house. She had taken me to the roof to admire the view when, from somewhere in the attic, I heard a strange laugh.

There was no joy in this laugh. It was wild, low, and chilling.

"Who was that?" I asked.

"Grace Poole," said Mrs. Fairfax, "a servant. She sews in one of the upstairs rooms. Grace!"

A woman appeared. She was solidly built and red-haired, between thirty and forty, and I could not imagine that laugh coming from her.

"Too much noise, Grace," said Mrs. Fairfax. Then, having sent her away, she talked to me about Adele instead.

12

❦ ❦ ❦

The Horseman

I had intended to teach Adele all day in the library, but she did not have the concentration for it. I allowed her to play in the afternoons instead. She was lively and pleasant to teach, and Mrs. Fairfax was kind and calm.

I still heard the wild laughter from Grace Poole's room. Often I met her on the stairs, but she never made conversation.

On a chilly January afternoon I took a letter to mail in Hay, the village two miles away. It was a beautiful day of fading winter sunlight, and the paths were icy. At a fence I stopped to watch the sunset and heard, far off, the hoofbeats of a horse.

The lane was narrow and twisting so I could not see the horse yet, but I stood back and was waiting for it to pass when a sudden rustling nearby startled me. Gliding past me came a large black-and-white dog, appearing through the gloom as suddenly and silently as a ghost. It was a relief to me when the horse and rider appeared and galloped past, and I was about to continue on when there was the clatter of falling. Horse and rider were both down on the slippery path.

The dog, barking furiously, ran to me for help. The rider was struggling to get to his feet.

"Are you injured, sir?" I asked.

"Stand to one side," he muttered. Then he called, "Down, Pilot!" to the dog. With difficulty he limped to the fence and I offered help again.

"Thank you – this is only a sprain," he said, but he could hardly walk.

In the moonlight I could see his hair and complexion were dark, and his features strong and stern. He was about medium height, strongly built, and probably in his mid-thirties. If he had been young, handsome, and charming, I might have felt shy, but his gruff looks and manner did not worry me at all. He waved his hand at me to go.

"You are not fit to be left alone, sir," I said.

"Where do you come from?" he asked abruptly.

"From Thornfield Hall," I said. "I am on my way to Hay."

"You are not a servant, are you?" he asked, looking me up and down.

"I am the governess," I said.

"Ah!" he said. "The governess!" With a grimace of pain, he tried to move. "You may help a little, if you would be so kind."

He leaned on my shoulder, and I helped him to his horse. He mounted, thanked me briefly, and rode away.

It had been an exciting afternoon in such a quiet life. The idea of going back to Thornfield for an evening with Mrs. Fairfax bored me, and I lingered over the walk home.

Mrs. Fairfax was not in her room. Instead, sitting by the fire, was the large dog.

"Pilot?" I said, and he came to me to be patted. Leah came in.

"Whose is the dog?" I asked.

"Mr. Rochester's," she said. "He's just arrived, but he fell and sprained his ankle in the lane."

13

My Employer

Teaching Adele the next day was impossible. She was restless and fidgety, always finding excuses to leave the room so she could steal a look at her guardian. Mrs. Fairfax told me at last that we were to take tea with Mr. Rochester in the evening, and that I should wear my black silk dress.

Mr. Rochester was in the drawing room, sitting on the couch with one foot on a cushion. While he watched Adele playing with the dog, I took the chance to look carefully at him. His dark hair and eyebrows and strong features gave him a grim expression. At first he took very little notice of me, but then he asked, "You have been here about three months?"

"Yes, sir."

"From where?"

"Lowood School, sir."

"How long were you there?"

"More than eight years, sir."

"More than eight years! That would kill any normal person. It also explains the look you had about you when I saw you in the lane. I was sure you belonged to another world. Have you any family?"

"No, sir."

"Not of this world. You must be an elf, or something of the sort. Did your magical relations spread ice on the path?" Mrs. Fairfax looked up in astonishment.

"There are no elves in Hay Lane, sir," I said.

"Have you seen much of the world?"

"Hardly, sir, at Lowood."

"I have heard of Mr. Brocklehurst," he said. "Naturally all you schoolgirls were in love with him, am I right?"

"Certainly not!" I replied. "We hated him. In the days when he controlled the school we had thin clothes and were nearly starved. No, we did not love him. He terrified us."

"Did you learn anything at the school? Do you play the piano?"

"A little."

He asked me to play, so I did, but he soon stopped me, saying that I played not badly, but not well. He asked to see my drawings, and this time, he was impressed. He regarded them silently, with great concentration.

"Where do you get your ideas?" he asked me at last.

"From my head, sir."

"They are extraordinary. They are elfish. Put them away!" Suddenly he was dismissing us all from the room. I put Adele to bed, then talked to Mrs. Fairfax.

"Is Mr. Rochester always so changeable and abrupt?" I asked.

"I suppose so, but I never notice it now. It is his nature. His family did not treat him well, and he has had a troubled life."

She did not tell me anything at all about these troubles, and I did not ask. I felt I was not meant to.

14

The Fireside

Adele and I hardly saw Mr. Rochester for days after that. Occasionally he would give me a brief nod of the head if he passed me in the hall.

One evening he sent for us to join him in the drawing room. When he was last in France, he had bought presents for Adele, and they had just arrived. As soon as we entered the drawing room, Adele ran straight to the box on the table.

"Take your box, Adele, and disembowel it," said Mr. Rochester from his chair by the fire. "Just do it quietly! Miss Eyre, I cannot bear a whole evening in the company of a child. Sit down. I mean – please be seated. Oh, I can't be expected to speak like a dainty lady. Which reminds me..." He rang the bell for Adele's maid Sophie so that Adele would have someone to show her new treasures to. I was studying his face when he looked up and met my eyes.

"You were watching me carefully. Do you think me handsome?"

"No, sir," I said, without thinking.

"You look like a little nun, but you speak plainly!" he said. "What do you mean by that?"

"I'm sorry," I said, "I should not have said what I did."

"But you have said it," he insisted. "You must explain yourself. Do I look like a fool?"

"No, sir," I said.

"I need conversation tonight," he said. "I would like to learn more about you. Speak."

I said nothing. I was not going to talk for the sake of showing off and amusing him, even though I was his paid servant.

"I mean," he corrected himself, "please be so kind as to talk to me."

"As a paid servant?" I asked.

"Miss Eyre, you have great courage!" he exclaimed. "How many young governesses would have said that? When I was your age I was as good and innocent as you are. I have made mistakes since. I wish I had not."

"You could change, sir," I said, but he seemed to think it would not be easy. He talked and I answered as well as I could, though often I felt out of my depth. I was glad when the clock struck nine and I could go and put Adele to bed, but she and Sophie had left the room.

"Adele," he said, "has gone to change into the new pink frock she found in her box. She will come back soon, looking like a miniature version of her mother."

Adele arrived, dancing with delight in her frothy pink dress. "I look like my mother, don't I, Mr. Rochester?"

"Precisely," he said, and turned to me. "I will tell you about her mother one day. Good night."

15

※ ※ ※

Danger

Some days later, when we were in the gardens watching Adele playing with Pilot, he told me about her mother. She was Celine Varens, a French dancer, and he had been passionately in love with her. He had provided her with carriages, servants, and all the fine clothes she could want until he found out that he was not her only love. While she swore she loved him, she had been laughing behind his back with a young French nobleman. After that he had wanted nothing more to do with her, but he had agreed to take care of her daughter.

"She may be mine, but sometimes I wonder how I can love her," he said. "Do you still want to be her governess?"

"Of course!" I said. "She is most certainly not to blame for her mother's faults, or yours. As her mother abandoned her, and you wonder how you feel about her, she needs more than ever someone to love her."

Mr. Rochester had now been at Thornfield for two months, but Mrs. Fairfax said this was far longer than normal. That night I was lying awake wondering how long he would stay when I heard a strange, murmuring sound.

The clock struck two. Something brushed past my door.

"It is only Pilot," I thought nervously, but then there came a low, threatening laugh like the voice of a demon. Then footsteps. Terrified, but knowing I must wake Mrs. Fairfax, I slipped out on to the landing.

Two candles burned in the hall, and by their light I saw a blue haze in the air. Smoke was pouring from Mr. Rochester's room!

Flames were creeping along the bed curtains as I ran in. "Wake up!" I cried, shaking him. The smoke had dulled his senses, so I took the water jug and flung the water over him. As it quenched the flames, it woke him.

"In the name of all the elves in the world, Jane Eyre!" he cried. "What are you doing?"

I brought a candle as he put on his dressing gown. By the candlelight he looked around at the charred bed curtains while I explained what had happened.

"Stay here!" he ordered, throwing his cloak around me. "Wrap yourself in this to keep warm. Don't make a sound!"

He took the candle and left me in darkness. I was cold in spite of the cloak, and weary long before he returned.

"It was as I thought," he said gravely.

"Something to do with Grace Poole?" I said. "I heard her laugh."

"Grace? Yes. I shall sleep on the sofa tonight. Go to your room, and say nothing about this to anyone."

"Good night, sir," I said, but he seemed surprised.

"You have saved my life," he said. "How can you walk away like a stranger? At least shake my hand."

He held out his hand, and I took it. He seized my hand in both of his.

"I knew you would do me good," he said wildly. "When I first saw you…" he paused, as if he struggled for words, "it was in your eyes, my cherished preserver, good night!"

"I am glad I was awake," I said.

He stared at me without speaking.

"I am cold, sir."

"So you are! You must go!" He let go of my fingers very slowly, and I returned to my room too shaken to sleep.

16

❧ ❧ ❧

The Next Day

In the morning Adele's lessons continued as if nothing had happened, but the servants were at work cleaning Mr. Rochester's room and changing the bed curtains. Everyone seemed to think the fire had been caused by a candle left in the bedroom. I went in to hear what they were saying – and there was Grace Poole, calmly sewing on curtain rings!

"Good morning, Grace," I said, wondering how she could explain all this. "What happened in here?"

"Master fell asleep with the candle still burning," she said. "Luckily he woke and put out the fire with water from the jug. Did you hear nothing, miss?"

"Only a laugh," I said.

"I hope you bolt your door at night," she said primly. "It's safest to."

Her calm show of innocence amazed me, and I could not understand why Mr. Rochester kept this dangerous woman at Thornfield. I was determined to ask him; I knew him well enough by now to do that.

The way he had looked at me that night was in my mind all day. I found myself reliving it all, so that I hardly concentrated on lessons any more than Adele did. In the evening there was no sign of him. I joined Mrs. Fairfax for tea.

"Mr. Rochester has had a good day for traveling," she remarked.

"Traveling?" I said.

"Oh, yes!" She settled herself down for a cozy gossip. "He went first thing this morning to Mr. Eshton's house on the other side of Millcote. He will stay for at least a week. All the gentry are gathering there, and he is a great favorite with the ladies."

"Will there be many ladies?" I asked.

"Oh, yes, and he is very popular with them. He may not be handsome, but he is a rich and well-educated man, and that counts for a great deal. The Eshton girls like him, and there's Blanche Ingram, Lord Ingram's daughter. What a beauty she is! She and Mr. Rochester sing duets together. They both have fine voices."

"Does Mr. Rochester like her, do you think?" I asked.

"Maybe, but he is nearly forty and she is twenty-five," she said.

So Blanche Ingram was twenty-five, beautiful, accomplished, and the daughter of a lord. I was a plain eighteen-year-old governess with no family and no money. As soon as I could, I went to my room and shut the door.

Since the fire, I had imagined that Mr. Rochester might love me. Looking at my plain face in the mirror, I knew it had been a silly daydream. Just because he took a polite interest

and talked to me, I had thought he liked me, but he would marry a charming noblewoman like Blanche Ingram. Certainly not me.

17

Blanche Ingram

He was away for two weeks. I tried not to think of him and failed. When a letter arrived for Mrs. Fairfax during breakfast, my hand shook so badly I could hardly hold my cup.

"He will be here in three days," she said, "bringing all the fine company with him. I shall have to employ extra help to prepare the bedrooms!"

The entire household worked frantically for three days. Adele was delighted, bouncing on the beds and longing for the company to arrive. As we all worked together I sometimes heard the servants discussing Grace Poole, and what good wages she earned, but they always stopped when they realized I was there.

On Thursday evening the horses and carriages began to rumble up the drive, with Mr. Rochester riding his black horse, Mesrour. A lady rode beside him, dressed in purple, her rich black curls streaming behind her.

"Miss Ingram!" said Mrs. Fairfax.

Adele was longing to meet the fine company, but that night she had to be content with sitting on the stairs and peeking at the ladies in their silks and satins. The next evening, we were summoned to the drawing room. With Adele in

her pink satin frock, we waited there until the doors opened and the ladies flocked in with a waft of white silk and perfume.

Blanche Ingram, tall and dark, stood out among them. Adele stepped forward with a perfect curtsy.

The ladies all fussed over her, and Miss Ingram called her a "little doll," but I did not like the way she looked at Adele. There was a mocking air about her. She was much more interested in flirting with Mr. Rochester. Keeping out of the way in a quiet corner, I heard her speaking to him.

"You've employed a governess?" she said. "I can't think why, when you could send the child away to school. My sister and I had dozens of governesses and we teased them terribly. We usually managed to get them sent away. Shall we sing, Mr. Rochester?"

They sang together very beautifully. Her piano playing was excellent and she enjoyed admiration, especially Mr. Rochester's.

I could bear no more. I slipped out, sure that nobody would notice me, but in the hall I came face to face with Mr. Rochester.

"Why did you avoid me this evening?" he asked, looking into my eyes.

"I did not wish to interrupt, sir."

"Are you well? You look pale."

"I am very well, sir."

"Come back to the drawing room," he said. "You are deserting us too early."

"I am tired, sir."

"And depressed?"

"No, sir."

"Yes, you are," he said. "You are near to tears." It was true, and I could not stop a tear from falling as he spoke. "You may go, but you must come to the drawing room every evening. I insist. Good night, my..." Then he stopped, bit his lip, and left me.

18

The Stranger

Thornfield was suddenly full of life and bustle. During evenings in the drawing room, I was able to observe Blanche Ingram. She seemed bright, but she had no ideas of her own. She only repeated what she had read in books, and she could be spiteful to Adele. She would push the child away with sharp words, and order her from the room. I was sure Mr. Rochester saw through her and did not love her, but she was a suitable bride for a country gentleman. He did not love her – she did not charm him – but he would marry her.

On a wet afternoon when Mr. Rochester was out, a stranger arrived at Thornfield, a tall, well-mannered man who told us that his name was Mason.

He was, he said, an old friend of Mr. Rochester and had just arrived from the West Indies. They had known each other there; until then I had no idea that Mr. Rochester had traveled so far. Mr.

Mason had a lazy air about him, and he complained of feeling the cold.

The servant, coming to put coal on the fire, told us that an old gypsy woman had called at the house offering to tell the young ladies their fortunes. She was, he said, waiting in the library.

"She like looks a rough one," he warned them, but Miss Ingram ordered him to be quiet. The ladies were determined to have their fortunes read, and Blanche Ingram was the first to go to the gypsy. She came back declaring that the old woman was a tinker and a fraud who should be put in the stocks. Whatever the gypsy had told her, she had not liked it She was moody and cross all evening.

The other ladies took their turn and came back giggling. Then Sam, the servant, came to me.

"The gypsy says that there is another young lady in the house who must go to her. Will you go, miss?"

I was full of curiosity by now. "Of course I will, Sam," I said, and went to the library.

19

The Gypsy

There were no candles in the library, but by the firelight I could see the gypsy woman.

She sat wrapped in a cloak, with a large hat shielding her dark face and an unlit pipe in her mouth.

"Do you want your fortune told?" she demanded.

"I really don't care," I said. "I don't believe in fortune-telling."

"You are a difficult customer," she said. "Why don't you tremble?"

"I'm not cold."

"Why aren't you pale?"

"I'm not sick."

"Why don't you ask me about your future?"

"I'm not silly," I said, and she gave a shrill, cackling laugh.

"But you are lonely. You are not loved, and you do not try to be loved, but you are very close to happiness. Cross my palm with silver!"

I paid her a shilling. She examined my hand while I tried to see her face, but the room was too dark to make out anything.

"I know you sit alone by the window while the young ladies charm the gentlemen. Mr. Rochester has been charmed by a very beautiful lady. Have you seen love in his eyes?"

"I came to seek information, not to give it," I said. "Will Mr. Rochester marry Miss Ingram?"

"Yes," the gypsy said, "and they should be happy, but I think I have disappointed Miss Ingram. I let her know that Mr. Rochester might not be as wealthy as she thought. If a richer admirer comes along, he's lost her."

"I came to hear my own fortune, not his," I answered.

"You should speak much and laugh often," she muttered, "but you would rather do what is right than be happy at any price. You are ruled by your conscience and self-control, and without them, you will never be happy."

What was happening? Her voice was changing.

"I want smiles for you, not sorrow," continued the voice. "I can say no more tonight."

Suddenly I recognized that hand.

"Leave me, Miss Eyre," said the gypsy. "The play is over."

"Mr. Rochester!" I cried as he took off the bonnet and cloak. "You have been trying to make me talk nonsense! This is unfair!"

"Forgive me, Jane," he said, standing up.

"Only if I have not said anything silly. May I go now?"

"Tell me what has been happening in the drawing room."

"They were talking about the gypsy. Oh, and a visitor has arrived, a Mr. Mason."

His smile vanished. There was a gasp, and he said, "Mason!" He looked ill and had to sit down.

"Can I help, sir?" I said. "I'd give my life to help you."

"If I do need help, Jane," he said, "I promise I'll ask you. Fetch me some water, please, and tell me what is happening in there."

In the drawing room I found everyone, including Mr. Mason, talking and laughing. I reported this back to Mr. Rochester.

"Jane, if all those people came and spat at me, what would you do?"

"Turn them out of the house, sir," I said.

He smiled. "Tell Mr. Mason I am here, and show him in."

I took Mr. Mason to him and left. Later, when I had gone to bed, I heard him showing Mr. Mason to a room.

20

The Cry

Great heavens! What a cry!

The most appalling scream tore through the night. From the room above me came a tremendous commotion of banging and stamping, and a voice called, "Help! Rochester!"

Footsteps ran along the gallery. I dressed quickly and left my room. As I came out, doors opened all over the landing. Our visitors hurried around with candles, demanding to know what was happening, and when Mr. Rochester appeared all the ladies ran to him.

"Leave me," he said firmly. "There is no need for panic. A servant had a nightmare, that's all. Please go back to bed."

By coaxing and insisting he persuaded them all back to their rooms. I went to mine, but I stayed ready in case I was needed, and, after a long wait, I heard a knock at the door.

"Are you up and dressed?" It was Mr. Rochester.

"Yes, sir."

"Come quietly, then," he said. "Bring a sponge and smelling salts." When I emerged, he asked, "Do you get sick at the sight of blood?"

"I don't think so, sir," I said, and he led me to a room on the third floor. I recognized it and shivered. It was the room next to Grace Poole's.

Mr. Mason was drooped in a chair. His face was ghostly white. His arm and shoulder were bandaged and bleeding. Mr. Rochester bathed the wound with my sponge and held my smelling salts under Mr. Mason's nose until he moaned and opened his eyes.

"Courage, Richard, courage," said Mr. Rochester. "I'm going for a doctor, Jane, so stay here until I come back. Wash away the blood. Use the smelling salts if he faints. You must not speak to him. Richard, you must not speak to her."

He left, locking the door. In the dark of night, I was locked in with a fainting and bleeding patient and only one door between Grace Poole and myself. All night I bathed away the blood, alert to every sound. In the next room, something creaked. What was it about Grace Poole, that she was capable of fire-starting and savagery, but was still kept here? Why was Mr. Mason up here at all, and why was everything so secret? And why had Mr. Rochester been stunned by his arrival?

I feared Mr. Mason was dying. It was dawn, and my candle had burned out before Mr. Rochester and the doctor arrived.

"She's done me in," moaned Mr. Mason.

"You're in no danger," said the doctor, "but these are tooth marks!"

"She said she'd drain my blood," whispered Mr. Mason.

"We'll get you away for your sake and hers," said Mr. Rochester grimly. "I told you not to go near her." When the wound was dressed and Mr. Mason looked a little better, Mr. Rochester helped him outside to the doctor's carriage.

After Mr. Mason had gone, we walked back through the gardens. Mr. Rochester cut an early rose from one of the bushes for me.

"Were you afraid when I left you?" he asked.

"Only of Grace Poole, sir," I said.

"She won't harm you. I would never have left you in danger, but I am in danger myself, until Mason leaves England. With a word, he could deprive me of all happiness. Jane, will you sit up with me the night before I am married?"

"Yes, sir," I said.

"Blanche is lovely, isn't she, Jane?"

"Yes, sir," I said. I had to face the truth.

21

Mrs. Reed

The next day, a messenger arrived for me. It was Bessie's husband, Robert, the coachman from Gateshead Hall. He was wearing black for mourning, and I asked who it was for.

"Your cousin John Reed is dead," he said. "He lived a wild life for years, in and out of debt, in and out of prison. He ran through his own money and much of his mother's, and when she refused to give him any more, he took his own life. The shock was so bad that she had a stroke, and she's now very ill. She's asking for you, Miss Jane."

I found Mr. Rochester playing billiards with Blanche Ingram, who scowled when I asked to speak to him alone. He threw down his cue and followed me from the room.

"My aunt is very ill," I explained. "I must go to her, sir."

"You said you had no relations," he said.

"None that wanted me," I said.

"But she wants you now?" he replied, so I explained the circumstances to him.

"Well, you must go," he agreed reluctantly, "but only for a week." He gave me money for my expenses and went on making conversation and saying good-bye for so long that I thought I should never get to my packing. At last the dinner bell rang, and I was able to escape.

At Gateshead I was greeted warmly by Bessie and coldly by Georgiana and Eliza. Bessie took me to my aunt's bedroom.

She looked as stern as ever, but she lay helplessly on the pillows. Time had made me able to forgive, and I no longer hated her. I spoke gently to her, but when at last she began to talk, it was as if I was not there.

"I hated Jane Eyre," she said. "I hated her more than anything in the world. I should never have been asked to take her. She was so troublesome. My husband thought more of her than he did of his own children. Where is John?"

For several days she lay confused. I kept myself busy with my drawings while my cousins complained and quarreled. After two weeks, she sent for me again.

"Are you Jane Eyre?" she said. "I am dying, and there are things I must tell you. In my dresser, you will find a letter."

I found it. It was dated three years earlier. It read as follows:

Madam,

Please send me the address of my niece, Jane Eyre. I would like her to join me here in Madeira. Having become rich, and with no children of my own, I intend to adopt her as my heir.

It was signed, "John Eyre."

"Why did you not tell me?" I asked.

"Because I hated you," she said. "I could not bear the way you spoke to me! I told him you had died of typhoid at Lowood."

It was too late to be angry. I forgave her, fully and freely, but I think she could never forgive me. Her habit of hating me was too hard to break. She died at midnight.

22
❦ ❦ ❦
Back to Thornfield

It was a long, slow journey from Gateshead Hall to Millcote. This time there was no carriage waiting for me, but I did not mind. I enjoyed the spring evening walk to Thornfield Hall. Mr. Rochester would not be thinking of me at all, but at least I would soon be with him again.

As I reached the house, I saw him. I found myself trembling and so unsure of myself that I turned to go in by another way, but it was too late – he had seen me.

"Jane!" he cried. "You should have sent for the carriage instead of slipping along here like a dream! Why have you been away so long?"

"I stayed until my aunt died, sir," I said, hoping my face did not give away how glad I was to see him.

"So you reappear by twilight like a ghost from the land of the dead! I always said you were an elfin creature. You've forgotten all about me, I'm sure," he said, and sounded as if he really cared whether I remembered him. "I have bought a new carriage, Jane, for my bride. I just wish I could look as splendid in it as she will. You are magical – can you give me a charm to make me handsome?"

"It would be past the power of magic, sir," I said, though he was handsome enough to me. He gave me a rare smile and walked with me to the house, and I found myself saying, "It's so good to be home! Wherever you are is home to me."

I should not have said that, but I couldn't help it. I hurried away ahead of him and was welcomed with joy by Adele and Mrs. Fairfax.

The next two weeks were quiet. To my surprise, there was no mention of the approaching wedding and no preparation for it. Mr. Rochester never even went to Ingram Park. I wondered if Miss Ingram had changed her mind about him, but he didn't seem upset. Indeed, he seemed unusually happy and spoke to me far more than ever before. More than ever he was kind, and more than ever I loved him.

23

❦ ❦ ❦

Midsummer Eve

Midsummer was radiantly sunny. On the long, warm evening of midsummer day when the sun was setting, I went for a walk in the orchard. The air was fragrant with flowers, but another scent lingered too.

It was Mr. Rochester's soap. He was walking into the orchard. I would have slipped quietly away, but he saw me.

"It's a shame to go indoors on such an evening," he said. "Are you enjoying Thornfield in summer?"

"Very much, sir," I said.

"Have you become fond of simple Dame Fairfax and foolish little Adele?"

"Yes, sir."

"You do understand, Jane, that you must leave when I am married?"

"So you are to be married, sir?"

"You are absolutely right, as usual. As you know, Adele and the beautiful Blanche Ingram cannot live happily together under one roof. Adele must go to school, and I am trying to find employment for you. I have friends in Ireland who need a governess."

Such a long way from Thornfield, and from him! I struggled against tears, hoping he would not see.

"Shall we sit on the bench under the chestnut tree?" he suggested, leading me to it. "Come, we shall spend a last evening together. You will soon forget me and Thornfield."

"I cannot!" My self-control broke down, and I sobbed. "I hate to leave Thornfield! I have been so happy, I have met you, and I can't bear to be torn away!"

"Must you go?" he said suddenly.

"You have just said that I must!" I sobbed.

"No. You will stay. I swear it."

"You are playing with my feelings!" I cried. "Just because I am plain and poor and unimportant, do you think I feel nothing? I speak to you now as if we were equals. I wish you found it as hard to leave me as I do to leave you!"

"Jane, darling!" He gathered me in his arms and kissed me.

"You are nearly married," I said, struggling. "You are going to marry a woman you don't love. I wouldn't marry without love, so I'm better than you. Let me go!" I struggled free.

"Yes, Jane, you are a free woman," he said. "So choose freely now. I offer you my heart, my hand, and all my life."

This was more than I could believe. "You are laughing at me," I said. "Your bride is Miss Ingram."

"My bride is here. My bride, my equal, and my likeness. Will you marry me, Jane?"

It was too much to believe, and I could not find any words to respond.

"Do you doubt me, Jane?"

"Entirely," I said.

"You know I do not love Miss Ingram," he insisted, "and she doesn't want me, since I pretended that I am not so very rich. I love you, Jane. I must marry you."

In the moonlight, I examined his face. Truly, he was earnest and anxious.

"Accept me, please, Jane," he said. "Use my name – Edward – and accept me. I swear that I love you."

"Then, sir – Edward – I will marry you," I said, and thought I was in paradise.

He asked me, over and over again, "Are you happy, Jane?" as we sat together under the chestnut tree. Night fell, the wind grew strong, and the tree creaked and groaned. A storm was gathering, but we stayed there until thunder and lightning crashed. It was midnight when we reached the house.

"Good night, my darling," he said, and kissed me – to the astonishment of Mrs. Fairfax who was standing on the stairs. In the night he knocked at my door to ask if I was worried by the storm, but I was far too happy to worry about anything.

In the morning, Adele ran to tell me that the chestnut tree where we had sat had been struck by lightning in the night, and was split in two.

24

Preparations for a Wedding

After the stormy night came a beautiful morning, and I felt for the first time in my life that I was worth looking at. Mr. Rochester thought so too, when instead of his usual "Good morning" he took me in his arms and kissed me.

"Is this my pale elf," he said, "this lovely bright-faced girl? I shall send for the family jewels from London for you."

"I am still only Jane Eyre," I said. I could not imagine myself adorned as a great lady.

"Jane Rochester, in four weeks' time," he said, and the thought of my new name startled me. Somehow, it even made me afraid.

He suggested a quiet wedding, and a honeymoon in Europe. "Ask me for anything, Jane," he pleaded. "Please, ask."

"Then please do not send for the jewels," I said, smiling.

"If that is what you want, Jane," he said, "but it isn't asking for anything. Ask again."

"Then tell me a secret," I said. He frowned darkly for the first time that day.

"A dangerous request," he said. "I don't promise an answer."

"Are you going to make me plead and cry and sulk?" I teased him.

"Don't try it," he warned. "What do you want to know?"

"Why did you pretend you would marry Blanche Ingram?"

He relaxed, and smiled again. "Is that all? I did it to make you as much in love with me as I was with you. I wanted to make you jealous."

"That was cruel to her."

"Don't worry, she feels nothing except pride. Come with me to town. While you fetch your bonnet, I'll tell Mrs. Fairfax the good news."

It was not good news at all to Mrs. Fairfax. I went into her room later.

"Are you really and truly going to marry Mr. Rochester?" she asked. "He is ever so much older than you are. I hope all will be well, but I doubt it."

In town, Mr. Rochester bought silk for a dozen new dresses, but I insisted that I would not wear them until we were married. Until that day, I wanted us to be master and governess. I would teach Adele, eat with her, and wear the old dresses I had brought from Lowood. Mr. Rochester grumbled at this, but I knew he liked my independence and the way I stood up to him.

At seven o'clock every evening he would send for me. Soon there was less "darling" and more "provoking puppet" and "elf," the teasing names he had always used, which I liked much more. He was more likely now to tweak my ear than to kiss me, and this suited me very well. Intense devotion alarmed me, but as long as I teased him, he could not regard me as an angel.

Having at last learned of my uncle in Madeira, I wrote to tell him that Mrs. Reed had lied to him. He was the only relation I had, and I wanted him to know that I was alive, and about to be married.

Mrs. Fairfax changed her mind about our marriage when she saw how happy I made Mr. Rochester. At that time, he was all I cared about. He was my whole world.

25

The Veil

It was the day before our wedding. My boxes were all packed and ready to go to our London hotel, Mr. Rochester himself having written out the labels with "Mrs. Rochester," and the address. Clothes for "Mrs. Rochester" hung in my wardrobe, but as long as I remained Jane Eyre, I would not wear them.

I was restless and anxious that day, and Edward was not at home. When it grew late I ran down the road to meet him, happy to hear Mesrour's hoofbeats and see Pilot running ahead, and even happier to be lifted into the saddle to ride back with him. It was not only that I missed him. Something had happened the night before to terrify and disturb me.

We sat up late together in the evening. "You are worried, Jane," he said. "Has something happened while I was away?"

"It was last night," I said. "I had a night full of bad dreams about being separated from you."

"You are excited. Was that all?"

"When I woke there was a light in my room and I thought it was morning – but it was candlelight. Something rustled near the wardrobe. I had hung my wedding dress on the door with that beautiful veil you sent from London. I sat up, and I saw…"

"One of the servants?" said Mr. Rochester as I hesitated.

"No," I said, and shuddered. "It was a woman, tall and large, with thick, dark hair. She threw my veil over her head and looked in the mirror, and I saw – oh, the most horrible face! Discolored, almost purple, and savage! She had bloodshot eyes and swollen lips, and she glared into the mirror."

He was attending closely to all I said, with a frown of disquiet. "Then what happened?" he demanded.

"She ripped the veil in two, trampled on it, and took the candle away, but then she stopped. She saw me! She bent over me – that horrible face – I lost consciousness. What was it, Edward?"

"There's no question, Jane, it was the result of nerves, and nothing more."

"Oh, but it was real. The veil lies on my bedroom floor, ripped in two."

There was a gasp and a shudder from Mr. Rochester, and he threw his arms around me. "Thank goodness it was only the veil," he said, and he held me tightly.

"Yes, Jane," he said at last. "Grace Poole came to you last night, but because you had been having nightmares, you saw her as a specter. I know you wonder why I keep her here. A year from our wedding, Jane, I will explain."

I was not satisfied with this explanation, but I knew it was the only one he would give. It was late, and I wanted to go to bed.

"Jane," he said, "sleep in the nursery with Adele tonight. You should not be alone. Lock yourself in."

26

❦ ❦ ❦

The Wedding

Sophie helped me to dress, and she put so much energy into it that I hardly recognized myself, and Mr. Rochester was calling for me before I was ready. I remember wondering, as he hurried me to church, what made him so silent and grim. He strode forward so quickly, I could hardly keep up. There were two strangers at the back of the church, but he did not appear to see them.

We took our places at the rail. The vicar began the service and reached the part where the bride and groom are asked if there is any reason why they should not marry. We were about to make our vows when a loud and clear voice cut into the solemn moment.

"The marriage cannot go on. There is an impediment."

Mr. Rochester swayed just a little, then recovered his footing.

"Proceed," he ordered the vicar.

"I cannot do that," the vicar replied.

Mr. Rochester's only response was to take my hand. How strong his grip was! His eyes were wild and watchful.

The speaker came forward. He spoke clearly, calmly, steadily. "Mr. Rochester is already married."

My nerves tingled and jarred. I stood firm and looked into Mr. Rochester's face, which was set hard. He put his arm around me and held me close against his side.

"My name is Briggs. I am a lawyer," said the stranger. "Mr. Rochester, you were married fifteen years ago to Bertha Mason of Jamaica. I have copies of the marriage certificate."

"That may prove my marriage," said Mr. Rochester, "but not prove that my wife is alive."

"She was living three months ago," said another voice, and the speaker stepped forward. It was Mr. Mason.

Mr. Rochester shuddered, and his face darkened. Mr. Mason turned pale.

"Mrs. Rochester is my sister," said Mr. Mason. "She lives at Thornfield."

Mr. Rochester was silent for several moments. Finally, he spoke.

"Enough! There will be no wedding today. Yes, I have a wife living. When Mason's family tricked me into marrying her they knew she was gradually going insane. Her mother was a madwoman, already in an asylum, and the daughter was becoming like her. They hid all this from me. The scenes I have endured with her! Do I not have the right to break this ridiculous bond and seek a real marriage? Jane is innocent, she knows nothing of all this. Come with me!"

He led us all back to Thornfield and waved away the astonished servants, who had been waiting to greet us. Holding my hand, he took us to the third floor and unlocked Grace Poole's door.

Grace sat by the fire. In a corner, something on all fours scurried about. It snarled from beneath a wild mane of hair.

"How is she today, Grace?" asked Mr. Rochester.

"Snappy, but not outrageous, thank you, sir," said Grace. Then the creature reared up, screamed, and sprang at Mr. Rochester as he flung me to safety behind him. The other men retreated as he struggled with the powerful madwoman. With terrible strength she fought to choke and bite him. He would have struck her, but he would not. He grabbed her arms and at last, with Grace's help, tied her to a chair.

"My wife, gentlemen," he said with a bitter smile, and he laid a hand on my shoulder. "Can you blame me for seeking happiness with Jane?"

The solicitor turned to me. "I will inform your uncle," he said.

"My uncle? What has he to do with this?"

"Your uncle, John Eyre, knows Mr. Mason. When you wrote to tell him you were to be married to a Mr. Rochester, he told Mr. Mason."

I went to my room, locked myself in, and changed into my plain dress.

Sitting with my head on my arms, I was too stunned to cry. Misery overwhelmed all else.

27

Decision

I stayed there all day. When at last I awoke I knew that I had to leave Edward Rochester.

Standing made me dizzy. I had eaten nothing since the previous morning. I stumbled unsteadily out of my room and fell into the arms of Mr. Rochester.

"Aren't you angry, Jane?" he asked gently as he held me. "I have waited here all day, and you haven't made a sound. I never meant to make you suffer. Can you forgive me?"

Of course I could. I knew he meant it.

He took me downstairs and brought me something to eat and drink, and I began to revive. He would have kissed me, but I turned my face away.

"Everything is changed now, sir," I said. "You have a wife. I must leave."

"I was wrong to keep you here at all," he said. "Thornfield is tainted by that fearful hag. Do you no longer love me?"

"I love you more than ever," I said, and could not restrain my tears. "That's why I have to leave. I can't stay with you, knowing you are married to someone else."

"I don't regard that as a marriage. You shall be my wife, Jane. Come with me to my villa in France. You will be known as Mrs. Rochester, and I promise to be faithful to you as a husband. I will regard you as my wife."

"But it would be a lie, for I would only be your mistress. I cannot live that way."

"Jane, have pity!" he implored. With pale face and blazing eyes, he took my hand. "Listen to me, and you will understand everything."

He told me how the Mason family had tricked him into marriage and about the appalling life he had led with Bertha. Her unspeakable behavior had almost driven him to take his own life, but he had resolved at last to keep her at Thornfield. Years of travel had followed, but nothing had made him happy.

"Then I came home and found you, the tiny elf at the fence, offering to help me. You are the only true love I have ever known. Won't you stay with me as if you were my wife?"

"No, sir, because I am not your wife."

"Do you mean it?"

"I do," I said.

He took me in his arms and kissed me. "Do you mean it now?"

"I do!" I pushed him away.

"What will I become without you? This is cruel, Jane! It is wicked!"

"Have faith. You will survive this."

"How can you be so frail and so strong! Think of me, Jane!"

I tried to walk out, but with a cry he flung himself on the sofa, and I could not bear his passionate sobbing. I kissed him once more.

"Bless you," I said. "May you be rewarded for your kindness to me."

In the morning before anyone else was up I left Thornfield. I carried only what was my own.

I took the first coach that came, and I paid the driver all the money I had to take me as far away from Thornfield as possible. I knew the pain I would give Mr. Rochester by leaving him. That was the worst sorrow of all, and I hated myself for it.

28

The Moor

After two days the coachman stopped at a crossroads on a moor. I had no money to go any farther.

I didn't care which way I went, so I walked the moors until it was too dark to see. Then I ate the last scrap of bread I had and slept out in the cold. The next day I walked on until, exhausted and hungry, I reached a village.

I asked for work but nobody could help me, and my hunger became painful. I even trudged into the bakery and offered to trade my gloves for a bread roll, but they sent me away. I know what it is like to be a beggar, for I begged a little bread from a farmer.

I slept badly that night on the damp ground and spent the next day trudging around in the rain. Some cold porridge that was about to be given to the pigs was the only food I had all day, and at night I wandered to the moor. I thought I may as well die there as anywhere else.

In the distance was a light that could have been a house window. By then I only wanted to collapse on the wet ground, but I dragged myself to the light until I felt a garden wall and a gate. I staggered to the window.

I looked into a firelit room, peaceful and cozy. An elderly woman was knitting and two young ladies sat and talked. Something about their kind faces made me feel I liked them. When the old woman stood up and left the room I knocked at the door, and she answered it.

"What do you want?" she demanded.

"Please, I only want shelter and bread," I begged, shivering.

"We can't have a vagrant like you in the house," she said, "but you can have a penny to buy bread."

"I can go no farther – please, help me!" I implored, but she banged the door shut and bolted it. Suffering and despair defeated me, and I fell sobbing on the doorstep. I had neither hope nor courage anymore.

"I can die now," I said.

"Perhaps not yet," said a young man's voice near me. Then the speaker banged on the door and helped me to my feet. He took me into the warm kitchen, where I fell into a chair. One of the ladies brought me bread and milk, while the other took off my wet bonnet and, with concern and gentleness, asked me who I was.

"Jane Elliott," I said. They asked me where I was from, but I said nothing.

They left while I dozed by the fire. When they returned, the servant took me upstairs. She helped me out of my wet clothes and into a warm, dry bed where, blessedly, I fell asleep.

29

❧ ❧ ❧

Moor House

I lay ill for three days and came to know the people who took care of me. The young man was called St. John Rivers, and the young women were Diana and Mary, his sisters. The servant, Hannah, did not quite trust me, but the sisters were always kind and concerned.

On the fourth day I got up and found my clothes had been washed and ironed. A warm, earthy smell of fresh bread came from the kitchen, where I found Hannah baking. When she found me clean, tidy, and willing to help, she began to like me a little better.

She talked freely as she baked. I learned that the house was named Moor House and had belonged to the Rivers family for generations, but they were rarely home. St. John was the vicar of a parish called Morton, a few miles away, and lived there. Diana and Mary both worked away from home as governesses and were only back at Moor House for a short time. They were a close, loving family and the sisters, especially Diana, became my dear friends.

St. John was, I think, nearly thirty, tall, fair, and slender, and very handsome with an earnest, intense way of speaking. I was aware of his careful observation, as if no detail should ever be missed. He persistently asked about where I was from and who my friends and family were, even though the subject brought me close to tears. I felt I owed them some explanation.

"I have no family," I said. "I never knew my parents. My father was a clergyman. I lived with relations, went to Lowood School, and worked as a governess. I can't tell you why I left, but you must understand that I cannot be blamed for anything that happened. I left quietly and secretly, and if not for your kindness, I would have died."

"Leave her alone, St. John," said Diana. "Sit down, Miss Elliott."

I had forgotten about the false name, and did not answer to it. St. John noticed.

"Is that not your real name?"

"I dare not give my real name," I said. "I could be discovered."

"I understand," said Diana. "St. John, leave her in peace." He did, but not for long.

"What do you intend to do next?" he asked.

"Find work, and earn my own living," I said. "Will you help me? Any honest work will do. I don't mind being a servant. And may I stay here, please, until I find a home of my own?"

"You must!" said Diana.

"My sisters would like to keep you as a pet," remarked St. John, "but I would rather help you become independent." Then he returned to his book, leaving me exhausted by the conversation.

30

🌿 🌿 🌿

Partings

I came to love the wild moors, the little stone house, and my new friends, Diana and Mary. St. John was usually away. He worked with great energy, caring for the sick and poor and visiting people in all kinds of weather, but his hard work and devotion did not seem to make him very happy.

After a month, Diana and Mary were due to go back to their work as governesses. St. John had news for me.

With the help of a rich young lady, Miss Rosamond Oliver, he was opening a girls' school for the poor children of Morton. Would I be the teacher? There was a salary and a furnished cottage. I accepted at once.

"Are you certain?" he asked. "It is a village school, just teaching rough country girls to read and write. No French, no drawing, no music. What will you do with your abilities?"

"Save them. They'll keep."

"I intend to open the school next week," he said, looking steadily at me. "I think you will not stay long. You will grow bored with the country life. I do!"

"I am not ambitious," I replied.

The word "ambitious" startled him.

"But I am," he said. "Perhaps you have seen it. I preach contentment and humility, but I am filled with restlessness here."

Shortly before the sisters were to leave, a letter arrived that brought disappointment to all the family. Diana told me what had happened.

"Our Uncle John has died," she said. "He was our mother's brother. We never knew him because he and my father quarreled long ago and never made it up. We had hoped he would leave us enough for us to live here together instead of working away from home. He's left us nothing, though. The time may come when we can no longer afford to keep Moor House. Still, we are no worse off than we were before."

They took the news bravely. The next day, I moved into the school cottage at Morton, and Diana and Mary returned to work.

31

Rosamond

I found myself with a small, pleasant cottage and a school full of country girls. Some were rough, some were gentle, most had received no education at all, but all of them were teachable. I had a home and work and should have been happy, but I could not help comparing my village school and my new companions with Thornfield, Adele, and Mr. Rochester. I could have been living in France as his mistress, living my life with the man I loved so much. When I thought about it, though, I knew I would have felt guilty, ashamed, and dishonest all the time. I had more freedom as a village schoolmistress.

St. John called on the evening of my first day, as I was standing at the door of my cottage.

"My life here as a village priest has been wretched," he said. "It is not my calling. I know I was meant to be a missionary, and it is the thing I hope for with all my heart. I have vowed to leave, and go to the East."

His intensity troubled me. I was relieved when a bright, sweet voice interrupted us.

I looked up to see a very beautiful young woman, who introduced herself as Rosamond Oliver. This was the wealthy lady who had helped St. John to open the school. She was friendly and pleasant, and I liked her.

She bent to make a fuss of his dog, old Carlo, and as she did so a look of love and hope crossed St. John's face. By the time she straightened up, he was as reserved as ever.

"I hope you will come and visit my father," she said to him. "You rarely come to our home now. He is alone this evening and not very well. Will you return with me?"

"It cannot be a good time of day to intrude on Mr. Oliver," he replied stiffly.

"It is the very best time," she insisted, "and you must be lonely too."

She could not persuade him. She went away at last, turning twice more to look back at him.

So that was the way of things. She clearly loved him, and he found her fascinating, but there was no room in his heart for anything but his calling as a missionary.

32

The Portrait

Rosamond was rather like a grown-up Adele. We became friends, and she often came to see the schoolchildren, usually when St. John Rivers was teaching a class. She flirted with him in the hope of winning him, and I knew he loved her, but he poured his passion into his work.

I drew a portrait of Rosamond for her father, and St. John, when he came to call, admired it very much. I felt it would do him good to talk about her.

"You'd like a copy, wouldn't you?" I said. "I'll do one for you."

"I don't think I should have her portrait," he said.

"You should certainly have the original," I told him, meaning Rosamond herself. "She is a sweet girl. She talks of you continually, and she loves you."

"What a wonderful idea!" he said. To my astonishment, he took out his watch and placed it on the table. "Let us allow a quarter of an hour to talk of Rosamond. To be married to Rosamond!" Then he fell into a happy daydream of a future with her. After exactly fifteen minutes he put the watch back in his pocket.

"It is not to be," he said. "She could never be a missionary's wife."

"Then don't be a missionary," I said.

"My great work!" he exclaimed. "It is all I live for!"

"Poor Rosamond," I said.

"She will forget me, and marry somebody else." He looked again at the portrait. Then he cast a sharp, sudden glance at the piece of scrap paper underneath it. He picked it up, examined it, glanced at me, and tore a strip from the margin. He said good-bye and left in a hurry.

It made no sense to me. I looked carefully at the sheet of scrap paper, but I saw nothing interesting. Soon, I had forgotten all about it.

33

St. John's News

All the following day, snow swept into the valley and lay in drifts.

That evening, the door banged, and in blew St. John Rivers, wrapped in his cloak.

"What's the matter?" I demanded.

"Nothing." He took off his wet cloak and stamped snow from his boots. "I need to talk to you." Then he simply sat down by the fire and gazed calmly and thoughtfully into it.

Finally, he said, "I have a story to tell you. I recently heard about a poor curate who married a rich man's daughter, but within two years they had both died. They left a baby daughter who was brought up by a Mrs. Reed of Gateshead. You look startled, Miss Elliott! Perhaps you just heard a cat somewhere? The child went to Lowood School, then became governess in the home of a gentleman named Rochester.

"Mr. Rochester," he went on, "wanted to marry her, but she discovered at the altar that he was already married and his wife was insane. The governess ran away and has never been traced, although Mr. Rochester searched for her far and wide. It is now vital that she is found. A solicitor named Mr. Briggs has just written to me with all this information. Now, Miss Elliott, what do you think of this story?"

There was no point in trying to pretend any longer. He knew everything.

"Please, only tell me this," I begged him. "How is Mr. Rochester?"

"I have no idea; it is not my concern."

He took out a thin piece of paper, torn along one edge. It was the piece he had torn from my scrap paper. In a thoughtless moment I had written "Jane Eyre" on it.

"You are Jane Eyre," he said.

"Yes, but did Mr. Briggs say anything at all about how Mr. Rochester is doing?"

"Never mind Mr. Rochester. Mr. Briggs was looking for you because your uncle, John Eyre of Madeira, is dead. He was wealthy and left you all of his worldly possessions. Do you understand, Jane Eyre? You are a very rich woman – very rich indeed."

The only relation I had in the world was dead, and I had never met him. And now I was an independent woman!

"Why did Mr. Briggs write to you, of all people?" I asked.

"Oh, it is a complicated business. I will tell you another time." He looked embarrassed.

"Tell me now," I insisted. I placed myself between St. John and the door. "You must tell me," I said.

"All right," he said at last. "My full name is St. John Eyre Rivers. My mother's name was Eyre. She was your father's sister."

"You mean that my Uncle John was your Uncle John too! So you are all my cousins – you, Diana, and Mary!"

"Yes."

I had a family! The best, the most glorious, wonderful news! My friends were my family!

I insisted on sharing the money equally with St. John, Diana, and Mary. They protested, but I had my way. By Christmas I had shared out my wealth with my cousins and resigned from the school, and Diana and Mary were coming home to Moor House, this time to stay.

34

❦ ❦ ❦

Plans for India

Hannah and I worked with happy energy cleaning and refurnishing Moor House, making everything ready for Diana and Mary's homecoming at Christmas. St. John objected that I was wasting my talents and should do something more worthy than cleaning a house and making mince pies, but I enjoyed it so much! I had never had a home of my own before. Diana, Mary, and I spent Christmas in chattering, careless happiness, which must have irritated St. John, who could never be happy unless he was doing something useful. He was to leave England soon for his missionary work.

Miss Oliver, tired of waiting for him, was to marry somebody else. St. John threw his energies into learning Hindustani, which he said he would need when he began work in India. I started to learn it too. I had been studying German, but St. John asked me to learn Hindustani instead, to help him with his studies.

I did not object to this arrangement, but neither did I enjoy it. There was never any laughter with him, nor any freedom.

All this time, I had not forgotten Mr. Rochester. I had tried and tried to contact him, but no news came. I wrote to Mrs. Fairfax, but there was no reply. After two months a letter arrived for me but it was only a business letter from Mr. Briggs, and I was so heartbroken with disappointment that I broke down in tears. I was still crying when St. John asked me to read some Hindustani with him, and I could not hide my distress.

He did not seem surprised. He sat calmly back and waited for me to stop. Then he suggested that we should take a walk across the moors – he always took it for granted that I would do as he wished.

"I go to India shortly," he said, as we walked, "and you, Jane, have been chosen to come with me and work beside me. You are intelligent and hardworking, but not beautiful – a woman made for work and not for love. You are meant to be a missionary's wife."

"I know nothing about it," I said.

"I will help you. You will be extremely useful to me."

He talked and talked, trying to convince me that I must marry him and go to India, and I almost believed him. I had to forget Edward Rochester. I may as well forget him in India.

Still, I could not marry St. John. I still loved Mr. Rochester. And St. John did not love me – he only wanted a helper.

"I will go," I said at last, "I will work beside you, but I will not marry you."

"No, Jane, we must go as husband and wife," he said. "No other relationship would be right."

"We don't love each other," I pointed out, knowing that he wanted to rule and command me. "I could not marry on friendship alone."

"It is exactly what I want," he said. "We would learn to love each other after our marriage."

"I scorn your idea of love!" I said. "It is unreal and shabby, and I scorn you, St. John, for suggesting it."

We walked home side by side in icy silence.

35

"Jane, Jane, Jane!"

He stayed for another week and, by being polite and quiet, made me feel I had disappointed him terribly. When at last he was about to go, I knew we must part on good terms.

"St. John, you are angry," I said. "I hope we can still be friends."

"We are friends," he said, not looking at me.

"Not as we were. Will you leave me without a kind word?"

This time he faced me. His voice and face were cold.

"Will you not marry me?" he said. His chilled anger was terrifying. I was afraid of him.

"No, I will not," I said.

"Why not, exactly?"

"Because you do not love me," I said. "In fact, by now I imagine that you must almost hate me."

"Then," he said bitterly, "you will go by yourself to the mission field."

He still thought he should make my decisions for me, and I would not have it.

"I have no intention of going to India," I said. "There is still something here that I must do. Something worries me, and I need to put my mind at rest."

"You are wondering about Mr. Rochester," he accused me. He was right.

"I must find out what has happened to him," I said.

Scowling, he left me, and I hoped that this time, the subject was closed between us. We all ate supper together that evening, as usual, and afterward he came to me once more.

His persistence was wearing me down. Even as I wished him a safe journey tomorrow, he asked me, gently and kindly this time, to marry him.

"If I were certain that I was meant to marry you, I would," I said. At that he pressed his hand on my head and put his arm around me, and I felt he was claiming me as his own.

My heart was beating hard and fast. I found I had become completely still. I was waiting. Something – I had no idea what – something was about to happen.

"What is it?" asked St. John.

I heard a cry. It came from somewhere in the air, and it was wild, urgent, and full of pain.

"Jane! Jane! Jane!"

"Oh," I cried. It was Edward Rochester's voice! I tore myself free and ran to the door.

"I am coming!" I called out. "Wait for me! I will come!"

I flung open the door and gazed into the empty garden. "Where are you?"

My own voice echoed back. I sent St. John away from me, and this time he left without arguing.

I had found my own true strength now. I was so grateful that at last I knew exactly what to do, and I looked forward eagerly to the morning.

36
❧ ❧ ❧

Back to Thornfield

I said farewell to my cousins and left the next morning, full of hope and excitement. I was going back to Thornfield. Yes, I knew that Mr. Rochester might be away from home. Even if he was there, he was still married. Nothing had changed. I simply needed to see him again.

When we approached the house, I saw a ruin.

The house was blackened, roofless, and windowless. A darkened gap yawned where the front door had been, the chimneys had caved in, weeds grew between fallen rafters. Charring and soot showed that it had burned to destruction. Had it destroyed life too?

I had to know. I walked to the nearest inn, ordered breakfast, and asked the landlord if he knew what had happened at Thornfield.

"Oh, it was dreadful," he said. "It appears there was a madwoman living at the hall, locked away, and it turned out she was Mr. Rochester's wife. She escaped one night when her nurse was asleep, and set the house on fire. That was back in the autumn."

"Was Mr. Rochester in the house?" I asked, trembling.

"Oh, yes. He'd hardly left it for months. There was a governess there last year and they say he was out of his senses in love with her, but she ran away when she found out about his crazy wife. It seems the wife tried to burn him in his bed one night. She set fire to the governess's bed too, but that was after she'd run away."

"What about Mr. Rochester?"

"He traveled the country trying to find her, but she's vanished completely. He came back, sent his little ward to school, and found a new home for his housekeeper. Then he locked himself away at Thornfield. I never saw a man so changed, and all for a plain little governess."

"Yes, but what happened in the fire?"

"The whole place was going up in flames, and Mrs. Rochester was up on the roof, waving her arms and shouting. Mr. Rochester got all the servants out and tried to rescue the madwoman too – but she threw herself down to her death. Poor Mr. Rochester!"

"Is he alive?" I burst out.

"Oh, he's alive, but he might be better off dead. It came of his courage, the way he wouldn't leave until everyone else was out. The house collapsed around him. One hand was so crushed that it had to be amputated at once. He is also blind."

But he was alive, and I said a silent thank you.

"Where is he now?" I asked.

"At his other manor house at Ferndean, thirty miles away. Two of the servants, old John and his wife, look after him." I remembered John and Mary from my days at Thornfield.

"Can your buggy take me to Ferndean today?" I asked.

37

At Ferndean

Ferndean Manor was set in a forest. As I approached from the trees, the door opened and a man came out, holding out his hand to tell if it was raining.

It was my Edward Rochester. I stood silent and still, watching him. He stood strong and upright and his hair was still black, but brooding sorrow was in his face. He was a caged eagle. Presently, John came out and took him into the house.

I knocked at the door. Mary answered, remembered me, and welcomed me into the kitchen, where a glass of water had been set on a tray.

"Is that for Mr. Rochester?" I asked.

"It's all he has in the evenings now," she said. "He never wants supper."

"Let me take it," I said, but as I carried it to the parlor my hands shook so much I spilled half of it. Mr. Rochester was leaning against the parlor mantelpiece.

Pilot saw me, bounded up with delight to greet me, and nearly knocked the glass over.

I put down the tray and handed Mr. Rochester the glass.

"Is that you, Mary?" asked Mr. Rochester.

"Mary is in the kitchen," I said. He turned his head sharply. "Would you like more water, as I spilled most of it?"

"Who is it?" he demanded. "That voice! Who are you?" He stretched out his hand, and I took it at once.

"Jane's hand!" he said, and in the next second he had wrapped me in his arms. "Jane Eyre! My

121

darling, is this a dream? I have dreamed of you so much!"

"I have come back to you," I said, and kissed his blind face. "I will stay this time, and be your companion and friend – if you want me to."

"Jane, how can you spend your life nursing a cripple? Darling, you need to be free to marry someone else."

"I don't want to," I said. "I am a rich woman now, and my own mistress. I can make my own choices, and I want to be with you."

I persuaded him to have supper by telling him I was hungry, and we ate together. In his company, I felt we had both come alive again. Afterward I combed his wild hair, and teased him as I used to.

"Am I hideous now, Jane?" he asked.

"You always were," I said.

"Where have you been, you changeling? And who were you with?"

"I shall tell you tomorrow. I am tired," I said.

"Wherever you were," he said, "were there only ladies there?"

I laughed, and escaped to the room Mary had prepared for me.

In the morning I woke to hear him questioning Mary. "Which is Miss Eyre's room? Is she up? Does she want anything? Go and ask her." Later, we walked through the woods and I described the scene to him. Of course, he demanded to know where I had been and what I had done. I led him to a bench, where he sat me on his knee and I told him everything. He was most interested to hear about St. John Rivers.

"I suppose he was one of those plain, clumsy curates?" he said.

"No. He was handsome and well-mannered."

"Oh, was he? You don't have to sit on my knee, Jane, if you don't want to. What did you talk about?"

"We learned Hindustani together," I said, and stayed where I was.

"Why Hindustani?"

"He wanted me to marry him and accompany him to India."

"Jane, you can leave me," he said firmly. "Why are you still sitting on my knee?"

"Because I like to."

"No, Jane, your heart is with St. John," he said bravely. "You must go to him."

"No! I don't love him, and he doesn't love me. I'm unhappy in his company." I put my arms around him and saw him smile. "I want to stay with you."

"But I'm a wreck, Jane," he protested. "I'm like the lightning-struck tree at Thornfield."

"No. You are alive and strong. Plants will grow around your roots and in your shadow, and your strength will support them."

"Do you mean friends, Jane?"

"Yes," I said hesitantly. I meant more than friends, but was not sure how to say it.

"But I want a wife."

"Oh, do you? Then you should choose the one who loves you best."

"I will choose the one I love best. Jane, will you marry me?"

"Yes, sir," I said.

"Poor, blind, and crippled?"

"Yes, sir. I want nothing more in the world than to be with you."

"Bless you, darling! We must be married without delay! Instantly! This week!"

By this time, it was so late that Pilot had given up and gone home ahead of us for his dinner. But

Mr. Rochester still had one more thing he wanted to tell me.

"In these last few months, Jane, since you went away, I have learned to have hope. Last Monday, thinking that you must be dead, I hoped for my own death as well so I could be with you. Sitting by the window, lonely and ready to surrender, I called your name three times – "Jane! Jane! Jane!" Then I heard your voice, as if you were with me! I heard you call, 'I am coming! Wait for me! Where are you?'"

I did not tell him this at first, but it was the very night that I had heard him call my name.

38

🌿 🌿 🌿

Afterward

I married him, quietly, soon afterward – only the two of us, the parson, and the clerk were present. Returning from church, I went into the kitchen where Mary was cooking dinner.

"Mary," I said, "Mr. Rochester and I were married this morning."

"Well, of course!" she said, and went on basting the roast.

John grinned and said, "I knew what Mr. Edward would do, and he's done right. I wish you joy!"

That was ten years ago, and I know what it is to live with the person I love most in the world. He is my life, and I am his.

We often see Diana and Mary, who are both married and happy. St. John is still in India, doing the work he loves. I found an excellent school for Adele, and she did well there.

Edward and I are always together. We never tire of each other, and seem to talk all day long.

For two years he was completely blind, but in time he found sight gradually returning. He still has difficulty reading and writing, but he has some vision. So, when our first child was born, Edward was able to take the boy into his arms and see that our son's eyes were large, brilliant, and black, just as his own eyes used to be, and he held him with a full heart.

About the Author

Charlotte Brontë
1816–1855

Charlotte was the daughter of a Yorkshire, England, vicar. She was one of three sisters who became famous writers, although none of them lived beyond the age of thirty-nine.

When Charlotte was eight, she was sent with her sisters to a school for vicars' daughters. It was a very unhealthy place and there was an outbreak of serious illness. Charlotte's two older sisters died. Charlotte probably based the school in Jane Eyre on this place, and a character on one of her unlucky sisters.

When *Jane Eyre* was published, people found it shocking – but it became a huge success and is still popular today.

Pronunciation Note

St. John is not a very common name today. It is pronounced "Sin-jon."